Captain Cat

Inga Moore

CAPTAIN CAT loved cats. There were more cats on board his ship, the *Carlotta*, than there were sailors in his crew – which was why his sailors called him Captain Cat.

After a hard day there was nothing Captain Cat liked more than to settle down comfortably in his cabin with his cats. He would take out his maps and charts and study them, dreaming of wonderful places he longed to visit. Of course he had visited lots of places already. But these were mainly trading ports, because that's what Captain Cat was – a trader.

It has to be said that Captain Cat wasn't really a very good trader. Trading is a bit like swapping. You swap something you don't want for something you do. Only what Captain Cat wanted, more often than not, was a cat. Which was how he ended up with so many.

All the other traders laughed at Captain Cat.

"Just look at him," they would say, as they watched him hand over some priceless vase for another moth-eaten moggie. "Ha, ha, ha! No wonder he never makes any money!"

Then one evening, as Captain Cat sat studying his maps, he suddenly felt the time had come at last for him to see those wonderful places he had always longed to visit, and that if he didn't go now, he never would.

So the very next morning, when he left the harbour, instead of sailing east to the trading ports …

Captain Cat sailed west.

The other traders scratched their heads, wondering where on earth he was going. "Silly old Captain Cat," they said, as they watched the *Carlotta* disappearing into the distance.

For days Captain Cat sailed under a sky as blue as a periwinkle.

Then the wind stiffened. Inky-black clouds appeared over the horizon and a terrible storm blew up. Captain Cat had never known one like it. All he could do was to batten down the hatches and hope for the best, as the *Carlotta* pitched and rolled through the mountainous waves.

The sky was so dark it was hard to tell day from night or, for that matter, night from day.

By the time the storm was over, Captain Cat ended up miles off course. In fact, when he checked on his chart, to his surprise he saw he had been blown right off it – a good six inches over the lower left-hand edge.

Which meant that, while he wasn't lost exactly, Captain Cat now sailed on an unknown sea.

And he was just beginning to wonder if he would reach the edge of the world, when all at once he came instead to a remote and lonely island.

"Hooray!" cried the Queen of the island
when she saw she had a visitor.

And she rowed out to meet Captain Cat in her boat.

But, of course, not only did she meet Captain Cat, she met his cats as well.

Now, there were no cats living on that island. Indeed, the Queen had never seen a cat before.

"What dear little things!" she cried, and she insisted Captain Cat bring every one of them, along with all the handsome sailors in his crew, to the Royal Palace for a slap-up lunch.

The Queen's Mother, the Prime Minister, the Lord Chancellor and the Mayor – everyone who was anyone on the island had been invited to attend.

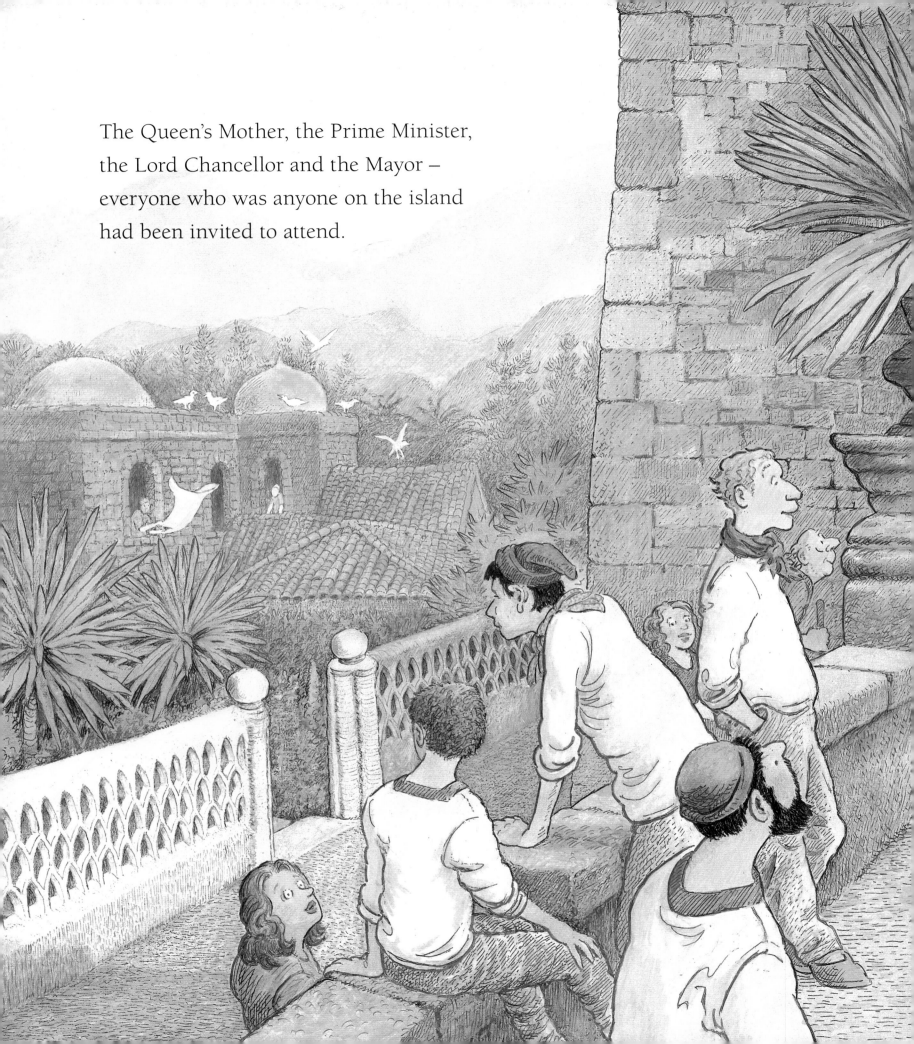

But no sooner had they sat down together and the soup was brought in,
than out from behind the skirting boards of the Royal Dining Room
popped hordes of hungry rats.

The Queen's footmen tried to fend them off, but the rats were too quick.
Up the table legs they shot, and in among the soup plates.

"Oh!" cried the Queen, turning bright red with embarrassment. "These horrible, horrible rats!"

"Don't you fret, Your Majesty," said Captain Cat, and he went outside to the Royal Courtyard where his cats were having fish for lunch.

"Why have fish," he said to them,
"when you can have …"

"*RATS!*"

Once they had got rid of the rats in the Royal Dining Room, the cats got to work on the rest of the Royal Palace, and when the sun set, not a rat was left alive there to see it.

"Oh, well done, you clever, clever cats!" cried the Queen with delight, as she inspected the neat rows of corpses lined up on the Royal Palace floor.

But it wasn't just the Royal Palace which was overrun with rats.
It was the whole island.

The Queen took Captain Cat to the Royal Treasure Chamber.

"See this," she said, waving a careless hand over sparkling
diamonds, pearls like ping-pong balls and rubies big as eggs.
"Take as much of this as you want. Take all of it if you like.
Only please, oh please, dear Captain Cat, let me keep your cats!"

So what did he do? Did Captain Cat give his cats to the Queen, in exchange for her fabulous treasure?

Well, yes he did, actually – some of her fabulous treasure at least, just enough to make him very wealthy.

But before you cry, "Oh! How could he? Didn't he love his cats?" let me tell you, it was the cats themselves who had the final say. They made it quite clear where they wanted to be, and it was not on the *Carlotta*. They had been living on that little ship too long, and after enjoying the freedom of the island where they could do what they wanted, where they wanted and when they wanted, they refused to go back on board.

"Won't you change your mind," the Queen said hopefully, "and stay here with us?" Both she and her Prime Minister had grown rather fond of Captain Cat.

But alas, Captain Cat would not. There were still those wonderful places to see he had always dreamed of visiting.

"Well, you know where we are," said the Queen.

And so, after one long, last, tearful farewell to all his cats, Captain Cat sailed sadly away.

But the story doesn't end here. Not at all. If anything this is where it gets really good. For without his cats Captain Cat found seeing the world wasn't much fun. So he sailed back to his home port where he began to unload his treasure.

"How did you get all that?" the other traders asked him, staring goggle-eyed at the sparkling diamonds, pearls like ping-pong balls and rubies big as eggs. And when Captain Cat told them, they very nearly fainted on the spot.

Then what do you think those traders did?
They sailed away to find the island for themselves.
For as they said, if silly old Captain Cat could
get such jewels there, just for a bunch of cats,
think what they would get for their fine wares.

Naturally the Queen was delighted to have the traders
turn up on her island with boats full of wonderful gifts.
Bangles and bracelets, necklaces, a new crown to wear,
fabulous silken cloth in every colour of the rainbow,
which she had made up immediately into ra-ra skirts,
one for each day of the week …

oil paints to paint with, books to read, curly-toed slippers, boxes and boxes of delicious, delectable Turkish delight, kites to fly, bicycles to ride – there was no end to the gifts the traders simply showered on the Queen.

"And to think they brought them all that way just for me," she said to her Prime Minister. "We must think of something really special to give them in return."

Which is exactly what they did.

The traders were waiting to load their ships with all the treasure they were expecting.

"I'm afraid your gifts are not quite ready yet," the Queen told them.

A few days went by.
Still the traders waited.

"Not long now," said the Queen.
And they waited … and waited.

"Nearly there," she said after another few days.

There must be an awful lot of treasure, the traders thought, if it's taking this long to count it out. And they imagined the piles of diamonds and pearls and rubies, getting bigger and bigger as the days passed.

Finally the Queen said, "Here we are at last."

But where was the treasure? There was none to be seen! There was only a footman carrying a basket.

"May we present to you," said the Queen, bursting with pride and pleasure, as the footman handed the basket over to the puzzled traders, "our gifts – the finest our island has to offer – these little gems, worth more to us than diamonds or pearls or rubies."

"Aren't they just adorable?"

And there, on a cushion in the basket,
sat six of the sweetest little kittens –
one for each of the traders!

Those poor traders could not have been more disgusted.

They took the kittens home and gave them to Captain Cat.
Which meant Captain Cat had his cats again – or rather,
his cats' cats – and then he felt like sailing more than ever,
and so he got to see those wonderful places, after all,
that he had always dreamed of visiting.

But not a single one of them measured up to the remote
and lonely island which, as well as being very beautiful,
was where his heart was.

And so, in the end, Captain Cat returned.

"Hooray!" cried the Queen and the Prime Minister
when they saw their old friend again.

And surrounded by his cats,
and his cats' cats and, later on,
his cats' cats' cats, Captain Cat
lived happily ever after.

*This book is dedicated
to cats everywhere,
and, most especially,
to my two neighbours
and tireless models,
Digit and Angus.*

First published 2013 by Walker Books Ltd, 87 Vauxhall Walk, London SE11 5HJ • This edition published 2014 • © 2013 Inga Moore •
The right of Inga Moore to be identified as author/illustrator of this work has been asserted by her in accordance with the
Copyright, Designs and Patents Act 1988 • This book has been typeset in Berkeley Old Style Book • Printed in China •
All rights reserved. No part of this book may be reproduced, transmitted or stored in an information retrieval system
in any form or by any means, graphic, electronic or mechanical, including photocopying, taping and recording, without
prior written permission from the publisher. • British Library Cataloguing in Publication Data: a catalogue record for
this book is available from the British Library • ISBN 978-1-4063-5557-4 • www.walker.co.uk • 10 9 8 7 6 5 4 3 2 1

WALKER BOOKS
AND SUBSIDIARIES
LONDON • BOSTON • SYDNEY • AUCKLAND